NOV 2023

The Swing

Britta Teckentrup

PRESTEL
Munich · London · New York

The Swing had always been there.

It looked out to sea and invited
everyone to take a seat.

It was a place to meet up ...

... and a place to be alone.

A place of joy, happiness, and laughter ...

... and a place for change
and big decisions.

A place of beginnings ...

... and endings.

The swing was a place full of life,
dreams, and stories.

Everything was possible there ...

Whenever Lisa sat on the swing,
she watched the clouds galloping by.

They took her
to faraway places.

Isn't swinging a little bit like …

... flying?

Mia and her grandmother walked to school
together every morning. And every morning,
they would stop at the swing.
"You can swing twenty times back and forth,
but then we have to move on!"
Grandma said with a smile.
They counted together:
"1... 2... 3... 4, 5, 6, 7, 8, 9... ...20!"
Then they both jumped off and continued
their journey to school.

When Mia walks past the swing today, she still counts
to twenty and thinks about her grandmother.
"You can swing twenty times back and forth, but then we
have to move on!" Mia says to her daughter and smiles.

The swing was a place to share secrets.

It was a place of rest.

It was a place to be free ...

... and see the world upside down.

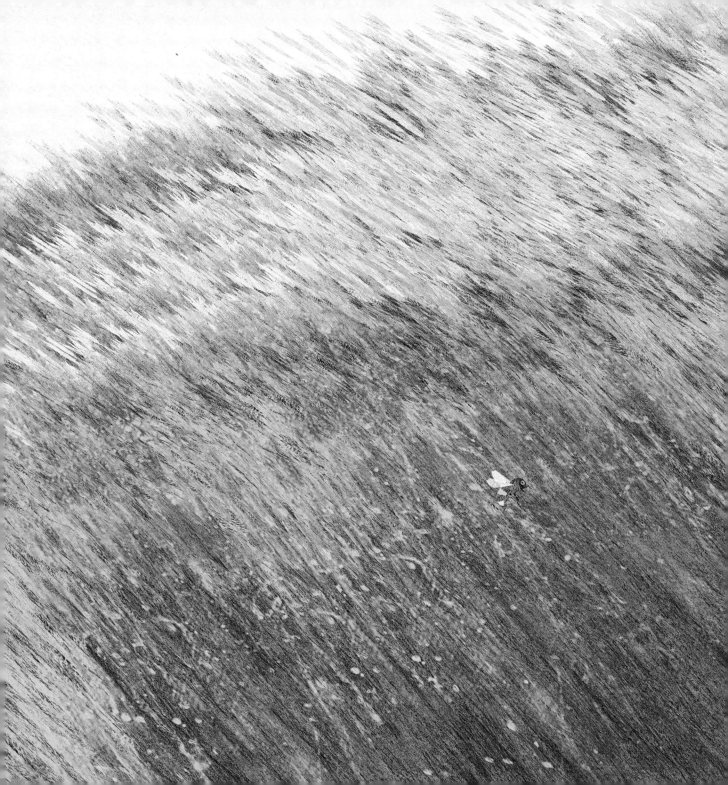

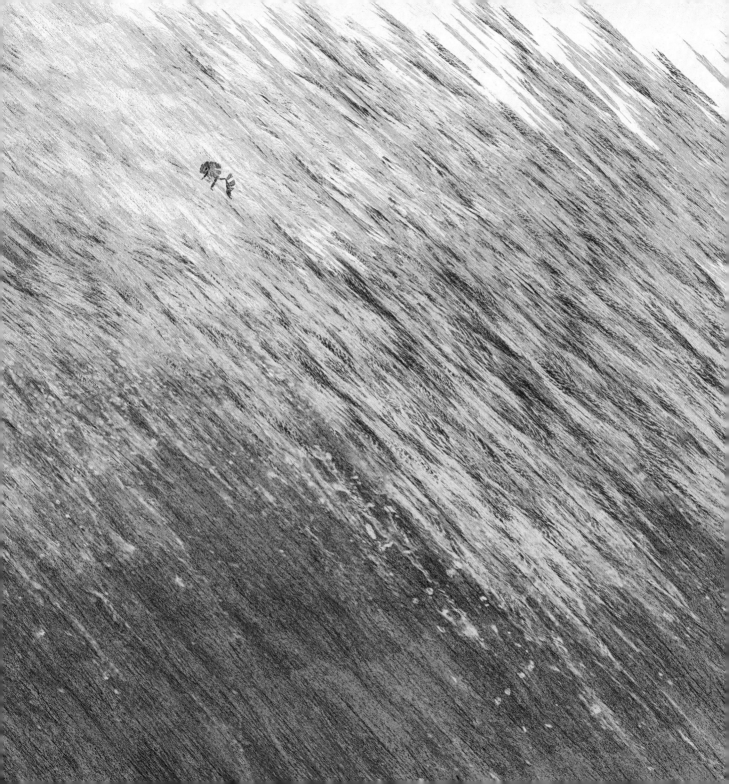

Sometimes sadness visited the swing ...

... but it never stayed for long.

When Jill looked out over the sea,
she imagined that the swing was right
in the middle of the glistening water.
"Doesn't the sea hold more secrets
than the sky?"she thought to herself.

The bright light made everything blur into one.
There was no beginning and no end.

Jill closed her eyes. She was surrounded by the sounds of the waves and the wind.

She felt that the secrets of the ocean were all inside her.

Summers at the swing were full of play ...

... and adventure.

There were endless parties ...

... and long, warm summer nights
when anything was possible.
Ella and Alex didn't notice that
the party had long since finished ...
They had too much to say to each other.

Sometimes there were storms and big arguments

where friendships fell apart.

Sami hadn't lived here very long.

His old home was very far away.

So much further than the horizon …

When he saw the vastness of the sea,

he felt a little bit closer to home.

The swing was a place full of memories.

Every Sunday afternoon, the old man visited the swing
and waited for the sun to set. He felt that his wife
was near. It was almost as if she was sitting on the swing
beside him, the way she used to do a long time ago.

He remembered her happy laughter and how
the wind had ruffled her hair.

The old man was always joined by a red cat that sat
on the empty seat next to him; together they watched
the sun go down.

When it was almost dark, the old man got up,
stroked the cat's head, and slowly walked home.

Many years ago, when Elias was little, he and his brother

would run up to the swing with their arms stretched out wide.

They were waiting for the five o'clock plane
to cross the sky. Elias loved planes, and he had
a little notebook where he recorded every
single plane he saw. "Higher, higher ...!"
he shouted, while pretending to be a plane.

When she was swinging,
Clara could feel her thoughts unwind.

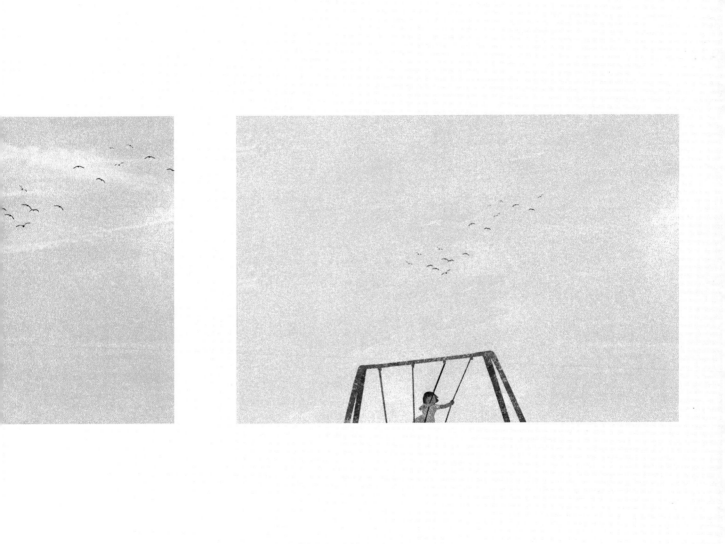

When Paula jumped off the swing,
there was always someone there to catch her.

In late spring, daisies and dandelions
grew all around the swing.

Every morning at six, Peter went for a swim in the sea.

He wanted to be the best swimmer ever!

When he came out of the sea, he took a rest

and thought about his future.

"I will show everyone what I can do!" he said to himself.

Peter was in no rush to get home—nobody was waiting

for him anyway. His father just laughed when he

told him about his dreams.

Finn can't remember much about
his grandfather, but he will never
forget that magical night they spent
together when he was just a little boy.
It was just him and his grandfather ...

They stayed up until they ran out of stories
and fell asleep under the starry sky.

They smelled the sea air and listened to the sounds of the night.

Finn always felt safe when he was with his grandfather.

Martha had an imaginary friend
who arrived whenever she needed her.

Many seasons came and went ...
And many years came and went.

On some November days,
the sea completely disappeared.

And sometimes, on particularly grey mornings,

the swing was taken over by the crows.

The days grew shorter and colder ...

... and on many days the rain wouldn't stop.

Max and Paul loved the autumn sky.

They would meet at the swing every day after school.

They still do.

In the winter, you could see the stars
in the middle of the afternoon ...

... and everybody waited for the first snow.

One day in March there was a raging storm.
The wind whistled and rattled, and huge waves
came crashing down. The little swing
was trying to hold on.

The storm lasted for two days,
and when the wind and rain finally subsided,
the swing wasn't the same anymore.

Nobody came to fix the swing.

Days,

weeks,

months,

and years passed ...

... until it was completely
overgrown and forgotten.

One day, a young man and his son walked past
the swing. The man had been travelling the world.
He was a famous swimmer and had won
many prizes, but now it was time to come back
to where it all began.
Peter was going to do things differently
from his own father. He picked up his little boy
and gave him a big hug. He started to clear
the swing of the overgrowth ...

When people saw what Peter was doing,
they all joined in. They worked together
and helped the best they could ...

... until the swing looked even
more beautiful than it did before.

The swing is still there. It looks out to sea
and invites everyone to take a seat.

It is a place of beginnings ...

© 2023 Prestel Verlag, Munich · London · New York
A member of Penguin Random House Verlagsgruppe GmbH
Neumarkter Strasse 28 · 81673 Munich
© Britta Teckentrup, 2023

Library of Congress Control Number: 2022935033
A CIP catalogue record for this book is available
from the British Library.

Editorial direction: Doris Kutschbach
Copyediting: Ayesha Wadhawan
Production management and typesetting: Susanne Hermann
Printing and binding: TBB, a.s.

Prestel Publishing compensates the CO_2 emissions produced from
the making of this book by supporting a reforestation project in Brazil.
Find further information on the project here:
www.ClimatePartner.com/14044-1912-1001

Penguin Random House Verlagsgruppe FSC® N001967

Printed in Slovakia
ISBN 978-3-7913-7531-1
www.prestel.com